MARVIN REDPOST

WHY PICK ON ME?

MARVIN REDPOST
WHY PICK ON ME?

Louis Sachar
illustrated by Sue Hellard

BLOOMSBURY
CHILDREN'S
BOOKS

Thanks to John Wagner

First published in Great Britain in 2004 by Bloomsbury Publishing Plc
36 Soho Square, London, W1D 3QY

Text copyright © 1993 by Louis Sachar
Illustrations copyright © 2004 by Sue Hellard
The moral rights of the author and illustrator have been asserted

A CIP record of this book is available from the
British Library

ISBN 978 0 7475 6282 5

Printed in Great Britain by Clays Ltd, St Ives plc

10 9 8 7 6 5

All papers used by Bloomsbury Publishing are natural, recyclable
products made from wood grown in well managed forests.
The manufacturing processes conform to the environmental
regulationsof the country of origin.

Dedicated to Judy and Paul

"What's your favorite vegetable?" asked Casey.

Marvin Redpost looked up. "Potatoes. No, carrots," he said. It was very important he told the truth.

Casey Happleton wrote it down. She sat at the desk next to Marvin. She had a ponytail that stuck out of the side of her head. Instead of the back.

"Casey!" whispered Melanie. "What's your favorite bug?"

Melanie sat in front of Casey.

"A stink bug," said Casey.

Casey Happleton was a weird girl.

"What's yours, Marvin?" asked Melanie.

"Uh, black widow," answered Marvin.

"Ooooooh," said Casey.

"Who's jabbering?" asked Mrs. North. "Marvin?"

"I wasn't jabbering," said Marvin. "Melanie asked me her survey question."

"Oh. Well, you can do that later," said Mrs. North. "This is silent reading time."

Marvin returned to his book. He was nine years old. He was in the third grade. Mrs. North was his teacher.

He liked Mrs. North. He liked the third grade. He liked being nine.

"Have you picked your survey question yet?" Stuart Albright asked him on the way out to recess.

"No," said Marvin. "I can't think of a good one."

Everyone in his class had to choose a survey question.

Marvin was supposed to ask everyone a question and write down the answers. Then he would have to do a report on it.

The results would be buried in a time capsule. It would be dug up in fifty years.

That's why Marvin wanted to think of a real good question.

"What was your favorite vegetable?" asked Stuart.

"Carrots."

Stuart nodded. "It's weird when you think about it," he said. "You have red hair."

"So?" said Marvin.

"They call a person with red hair Carrot Top. But really, carrots are green

11

on top. So they should call a person with green hair Carrot Top."

Stuart was Marvin's best friend. Marvin was the only one who understood him.

They got on line to play wall-ball.

"Hi, Marvin," said Nick, getting in line behind him.

"Hi, Nick," said Marvin.

Nick Tuffle was Marvin's other best friend.

"What's your favorite dinosaur?" asked Nick.

Marvin thought a moment. He didn't have a favorite dinosaur.

Stuart made a noise with his nose. "That's a stupid question," he said.

Marvin looked at his two best friends. He was afraid they'd get into another fight. Nick and Stuart were always fighting.

"What's stupid about it?" Nick demanded.

"Because," said Stuart, "the results are going to be buried in a time capsule. In fifty years people are going to dig up the time capsule. And then they're going to think there were dinosaurs around when we went to school."

"*That's* stupid," said Nick.

"Your turn, Stuart," said Marvin.

"What? Oh," said Stuart.

Marvin watched Stuart play wall-ball. He was up against Clarence, the toughest kid in the third grade.

Stuart lost.

Nick laughed when Stuart lost.

Marvin stepped up. Even though Clarence was bigger and stronger, Marvin felt he could beat him at wall-ball.

Clarence served. He bounced the red ball once on the ground, then hit it hard, with both hands together.

The ball hit the ground, then the wall, then bounced back to Marvin.

Marvin hit it with both hands. The ball hit the ground, the wall, then back toward Clarence.

Clarence smashed it. But too hard. The ball bounced off the wall and over the line.

Marvin caught it.

"I won!" Clarence declared.

"You did not," said Marvin. "The ball was over the line."

"You're crazy," said Clarence.

"I saw it," said Marvin.

"You did not," said Clarence. "You weren't even watching. You were picking your nose!"

Several of the kids on line laughed.

"It was over the line," said Marvin.

"Go pick your nose," said Clarence.

The kids on line laughed again, even Nick.

"C'mon, Marvin. Get off the court," said Ryan. "You're wasting time."

Marvin didn't move. "The ball was over the line," he said. "I saw it."

"You were picking your nose!" Clarence said.

"I was not!" said Marvin.

"You were snot?" asked Clarence. "He just said he was snot."

Everyone, except Stuart, laughed.

"That's not what I said," said Marvin.

"That's *snot* what I said," said Clarence.

"Just go to the end of the line, Marvin," said Travis.

Marvin didn't move.

Clarence grabbed the ball from him.

"Oh, gross!" he exclaimed. "His boogers are on the ball!"

Even Stuart laughed.

"I'm not playing with this ball!" said Clarence. He threw it to Marvin.

Marvin held up the ball. "Look, there's nothing on it," he said.

"Now they're on his hands!" said Clarence.

Everyone backed away from Marvin.

The bell rang.

The other kids hurried back to class, leaving Marvin holding the ball.

2

It got worse... .

After school Marvin walked home with Nick and Stuart. He was still upset.

"The ball was over the line," he said.

"Just forget about it," said Nick.

"It was over the line," said Marvin.

"We *know*," said Stuart.

"Then why didn't you say anything?"

"I don't know," said Stuart. "It was funny."

"Boogers on the ball!" said Nick, then he and Stuart cracked up.

Marvin didn't think it was funny. It was

unfair! Clarence was just being a bad sport.

"I didn't pick my nose," he said for the millionth time.

"Just quit talking about it!" said Nick. "Forget about it."

"You can't keep telling people you

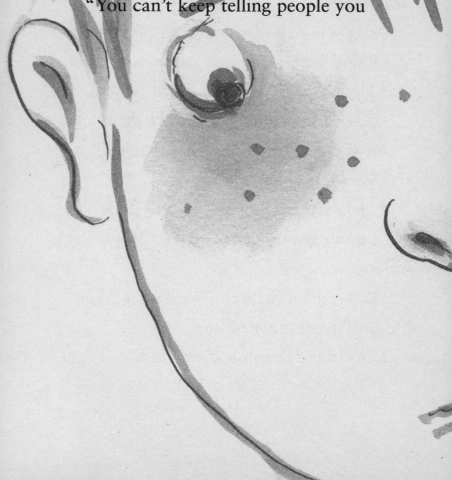

don't pick your nose," said Stuart. "That sounds weird."

"But I don't!" said Marvin.

His face burned as he thought about it.

Everybody had laughed at him. Even Nick and Stuart. If they were true friends, they would have stuck up for him.

He couldn't stop thinking about it, all day and into the night.

It was unfair. He didn't pick his nose. The ball was over the line.

When he got to school the next morning, the first person he saw was Casey Happleton.

"Hi, Marvin," said Casey. Her ponytail stuck out of the side of her head.

"I didn't pick my nose," said Marvin.

"What?"

"I didn't pick my nose," he repeated.

Casey looked at him a moment. Then

she remembered. "You're gross," she said.

Warren sat in front of him. He had been absent yesterday.

"Hey, Warren," Marvin whispered as he tapped Warren's shoulder.

Warren turned around.

"Did you hear I pick my nose?" Marvin asked him. "Well, I don't."

Melanie sat next to Warren. "What'd he say? What'd he say?" she asked. Melanie always wanted to know everything.

"He asked me if I knew he picked his

nose," said Warren.

"Oh, yeah," said Melanie. "Marvin's the biggest nose picker in the whole school."

"I am not!" whispered Marvin.

All morning Marvin kept telling everyone he didn't pick his nose. But the more he talked about it, the more the other kids teased him about it.

And the more they teased him, the more he kept talking about it.

"Don't get too close to Marvin," said Clarence. "Or else he'll try to pick your nose too."

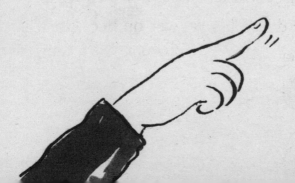

3

It got worse... .

"What's your favorite color, Marvin?" asked Judy.

Marvin thought about red, because he had red hair and his name was Marvin Redpost. But really, he liked green better—the color of grass and trees. The color of springtime.

"Green," he said.

"The color of boogers!" said Melanie.

"You're disgusting, Marvin!" said Judy as she wrote down his answer on her sheet of paper.

Marvin felt terrible. In fifty years they'll dig up the time capsule. And they'll find out a boy named Marvin Redpost picked his nose. And everyone will laugh at him.

Maybe in fifty years he'd be president! But then they'd dig up the time capsule and say, "You can't be president anymore. You picked your nose."

It wasn't fair. The ball was over the line.

They didn't let him play wall-ball at recess. "You'll get boogers on the ball," said Justin.

Everyone laughed. But it was more than just a joke. They believed it too.

As he walked away, he almost bumped into Heather. Heather was playing hopscotch with Gina. "Yuck, don't let him touch you," said Gina.

After school he caught up with Nick and Stuart.

"So what do you want to do today?" he asked.

Stuart and Nick looked at each other.

"We can go to my house," Marvin suggested.

"Uh ..." said Stuart.

Gina and Heather came toward them. Heather made a face at Marvin.

"Who's your best friend?" asked Gina. "It's for the survey."

"Nick," said Stuart.

"Stuart," said Nick.

Marvin couldn't believe it. Stuart and Nick would be fighting all the time if it wasn't for him. How could they be best friends?

"Who's your best friend, Marvin?" asked Gina.

Marvin looked at Nick and Stuart. "I don't have a best friend," he said.

He waited for Gina and Heather to leave.

"I don't pick my nose," he said.

"We know that," said Stuart.

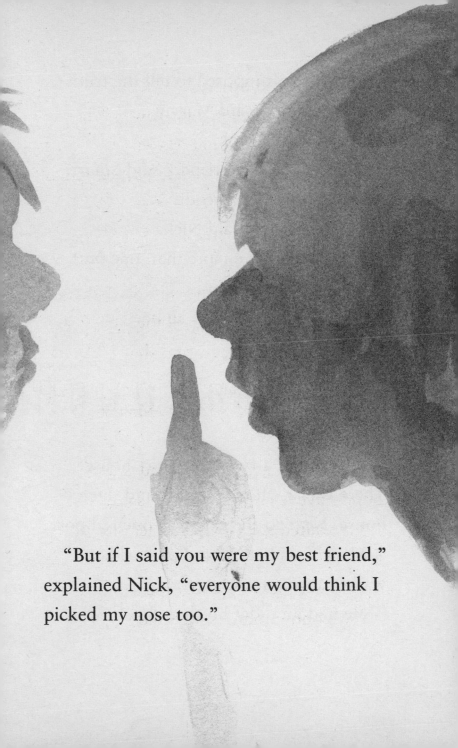

"But if I said you were my best friend," explained Nick, "everyone would think I picked my nose too."

"You were supposed to tell the truth for the survey," said Marvin.

"I did," said Nick.

"You're still our friend," said Stuart. "Just not our best friend."

"That's right," said Nick.

"You can't have more than one *best* friend," said Stuart.

Marvin walked home alone.

He lived in a two-story gray house. There was a white fence around the house. Next to the gate was one red post.

Marvin tapped the red post as he walked through the gate.

He had an older brother, Jacob, who

was eleven, and a younger sister, Linzy, who was four.

They were both in the kitchen.

"Marvin!" exclaimed Linzy. "Do you want to play Mommy-Daddy?"

"No," muttered Marvin.

Linzy always wanted to play Mommy-Daddy. The worst part was that Linzy

always insisted on being the Daddy. That meant Marvin had to be the Mommy.

"Hiya, Mar," said Jacob.

Marvin grunted.

"What's wrong?" asked Jacob.

Marvin shrugged. He couldn't tell his

big brother that the other kids said he picked his nose. It was so childish. Jacob was cool.

"You want to do something?" Marvin asked him.

"Can't," said Jacob. "Nate and I are going to ride our bikes down Suicide Hill."

"Cool," said Marvin. He opened the
refrigerator.

"Do you want to play Doggie?" asked
Linzy.

"No."

Doggie was worse than Mommy-
Daddy. Linzy would throw a ball, and
Marvin would have to fetch it.

He shut the refrigerator. There was nothing good to eat.

"Where's Nick and Stuart?" asked Jacob.

Marvin shrugged. "I don't know," he said. "And I don't care!"

He had better things to do. Lots of things.

"Okay, Linzy," he said. "Let's play Mommy-Daddy."

"Okay," said Linzy. "But I get to be the Daddy."

4

It got worse and worse... .

He did poorly in school. He always used to be one of the first persons done. Now there were times when he didn't even finish.

He didn't care.

Stuart and Nick had told him that he was still their friend—just not their *best* friend. But even that wasn't true.

"Why don't I see Stuart around anymore?" his mother asked.

"I hate him!" said Marvin.

"How about Nick?"

"I hate him too!"

Every day after school, he and Linzy played Mommy-Daddy or Doggie. Except when Linzy had friends over.

He thought about challenging Clarence to a fight. If Marvin won, then he didn't pick his nose. If Clarence won, then he did pick his nose.

But Clarence was the toughest kid in his class. There was no way Marvin could win.

"Look out! Here comes Marvin!" shouted Amanda as Marvin entered the lunchroom. "Don't let him touch you!"

He sat down at one of the tables.

Travis and Clarence came toward him.

"I have to ask you my survey

question," said Travis. "I've already asked everyone else."

"What?" asked Marvin.

"What's your favorite food?"

"Booger sandwiches!" shouted Clarence before Marvin could answer. "Marvin said he likes to eat booger sandwiches!"

Everyone laughed.

Mrs. Grant marched toward them. She was furious.

Mrs. Grant was the lunchroom supervisor.

Good, thought Marvin. *Clarence will finally get in trouble.*

But Mrs. Grant wasn't angry at Clarence.

"Marvin Redpost!" she scolded. "Stop that disgusting talk right now! You're going to ruin everyone's appetite."

"But I didn't—"

"Just stop it," said Mrs. Grant.

Marvin shook his head. He opened his
paper sack and took out his sandwich.

"He's going to eat it!" Clarence announced. "He's going to eat a booger sandwich!"

Marvin put his sandwich down. He wasn't hungry anymore.

"It's not a booger sandwich," he said. "It's turkey."

"Then why won't you eat it?" asked Heather.

Marvin sighed. He picked up his sandwich and bit into it. "There, see," he said.

"Ahhhhh!" screamed Heather. "He ate a booger sandwich!"

B.L.T
Booger, lettuce and tomato

"It's not a booger sandwich!" Marvin shouted.

Mrs. Grant grabbed him by the elbow and yanked him outside.

5

Worst of all… .

Mrs. North handed out report cards.

Marvin sat at his desk. He was afraid
to look. Slowly, he pulled his report card
from its envelope.

His grades weren't too bad. They
weren't as good as usual, but they weren't
terrible.

He only got one U. U for
Unsatisfactory. That was in Social Studies
because he never asked a survey question.

But then he read the teacher's
comments:

Marvin doesn't play well with others. The other children are offended by his unsanitary habits and anti-social behavior. He needs to learn to use a tissue.

He read the words over and over again. He couldn't believe it.

Mrs. North thought he picked his nose too!

It wasn't fair. The ball was over the line!

He put his head down and started to cry, right in the middle of class.

"Are you crying, Marvin?" asked Casey Happleton.

Marvin looked at her. Her ponytail stuck out of the side of her head.

"Why are you crying?" asked Casey.

"Marvin's crying!" announced Melanie.

"Probably picked his nose too hard," said Clarence.

6

Marvin walked home from school carrying his report card. He tapped the red post as he walked through the gate.

"Do you want to play Mommy-Daddy?" asked Linzy.

"No!" he snapped.

"I'll let you be the Daddy," said Linzy.

"No!" he shouted. "Leave me alone!"

Linzy burst into tears. "I'm telling on you!" she bawled. "You're not my friend anymore! You're not coming to my birthday party!"

Linzy's birthday was seven months away.

Marvin walked into his room. He sat on his bed.

How could he show his report card to his parents? They'd think he was disgusting too.

He felt himself start to cry. He sniffled back the tears.

"Even Linzy hates me," he muttered.

He sniffled again.

He had sunk as low as he could go.

He was nine years old, and his life was ruined forever.

And then he sank even lower.

He did something terrible.

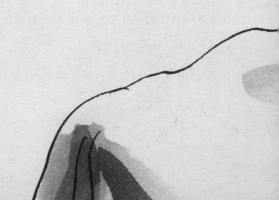

He didn't realize he was doing it, until after he had already done it.

He stuck his finger up his nostril, and picked his nose.

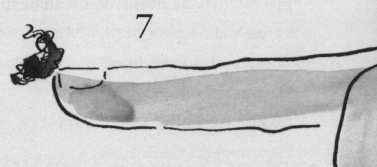

7

"Oh no!" he cried. "I'm disgusting! I'm as gross as everyone says I am!"

He went into the bathroom and wiped his finger with a tissue. Then he washed his hands using plenty of soap and water.

He stayed in his room all afternoon.

He stared at his report card, then turned to General Jackson, his pet lizard.

"Well, at least it's true now," he told the General. "I'm the most disgusting kid in the whole world."

General Jackson stuck out his tongue.

Marvin took his report card downstairs.

His family was in the den watching TV.

"Here's my report card," Marvin said, then threw it on the floor.

He walked out.

"Wait a second!" said his mother.

He stopped.

"Come back here."

He dragged his feet back into the den.

"Now what did I do?" he asked.

"Pick it up," said his father.

The report card lay on the blue and white rug.

"No," said Marvin.

"Your father asked you to pick it up," said his mother.

"You pick it up," said Marvin.

His mother stared at him.

He stared right back at her.

He didn't know why he was doing this. He got his parents mad at him *before* they even saw his report card.

But what could you expect from the most disgusting kid in the world?

Linzy picked it up. "Here, Marvin," she said.

He took it from Linzy and handed it to his mother.

Jacob looked at Marvin and slowly shook his head.

"Can I go now?" Marvin asked.

"No," said his father.

He watched his mother read the report card. Then she handed it to his father.

"What happened, Marvin?" his mother asked. His father was still reading it.

"Nothing."

"Something happened," his mother said. "I know you got in some sort of fight with Nick and Stuart. I thought it would pass. I figured you'd be friends again by now."

"We didn't get in a fight," said Marvin. "They just don't like me."

"Why not?" asked his father.

"Because I'm disgusting. I'm the most disgusting kid in school!"

His father read aloud from the report

card. "Anti-social behavior … Unsanitary habits. What did you do?"

"I picked my nose!" Marvin shouted. "I'm the world's biggest nose picker!"

Jacob cracked up.

"Sorry, Mar," he said.

"It's okay," said Marvin. "Everyone at school laughs at me too."

"Do you want to tell us about it?" asked his mother.

"There's nothing to tell," said Marvin. "I'm nine years old, and my life is ruined

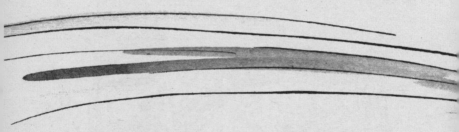

forever. Just because Clarence hit the ball over the line."

He told them what happened, from the wall-ball game up until his report card.

"Now even Mrs. North thinks I pick my nose."

"What about Nick and Stuart," said his mother. "Surely they must know—"

"They're afraid that if they stick up for me, then everybody will say that they pick their noses too!"

"Well, if that's how they feel, then they're not really your friends," said his father.

"Great," said Marvin. "I have no friends."

"Maybe we should talk to Mrs. North," suggested Marvin's mother. "And tell her you don't pick your nose."

"She won't believe you," said Marvin.

"The more you say you don't pick your nose, the more everyone thinks you do!"

His parents looked at each other.

"Jacob," said his mother. "You're close to Marvin's age. Has anything like this ever happened to you?"

Jacob thought a moment. "I remember when *I* was in the third grade," he said.

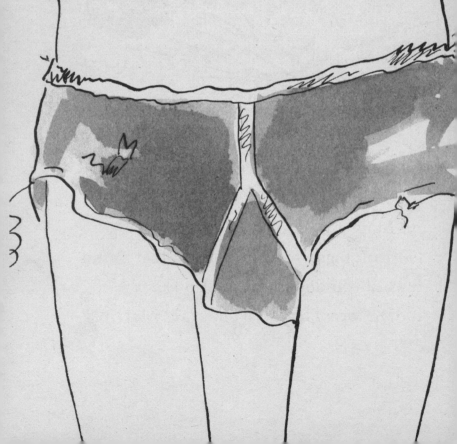

"There was this new kid. Larry
Clarksdale. Everyone used to pick on
him."

"What happened?" asked his mother.

"Uh, never mind," said Jacob.

"What?" asked Marvin.

"Well, I used to pick on him too,"
Jacob admitted. "I remember I once told
everyone that Larry still wore diapers. He
had to show everyone his underpants to
prove he didn't."

"That's awful," said his mother.

"I know," said Jacob. "I still feel bad
when I think about it."

"So what happened to Larry?" asked
his mother.

"Nothing. Everyone just kept on hating
him, all through third grade. Then he
moved away."

"Maybe they liked him at his new school," said Linzy.

"I hope so," said Jacob.

"We could move!" suggested Marvin.

"You don't solve problems by running away from them," said his father.

"Then what should I do?" asked Marvin. "I can't get into a fight with Clarence. He'd beat me up."

"I can beat him up for you," said Jacob.

"Okay," said Marvin.

"No," said their mother.

"Then what should Marvin do?" asked Jacob. "You two are supposed to be so smart."

Marvin looked at his parents.

They just sat there. They were stumped.

But then someone came up with the answer.

It wasn't his mother or father, or even Jacob.

It was Linzy.

And it wasn't exactly an answer. It was a question.

8

"Why is it bad to pick your nose?"

asked Linzy.

Marvin looked at his little sister. "It's a disgusting and gross thing to do," he said.

"Why?" asked Linzy.

"It just is," said Marvin. He was in no mood for Linzy's stupid questions. She could ask *why* a hundred times in a row.

"Why?" asked Linzy. "I pick my nose."

"It's okay when you're four years old," said Marvin. "It's bad when you're older."

"Why?"

" 'Cause it is!"

But then Marvin's father also asked, "Why?"

Marvin looked at him.

"What's so bad about picking your nose?" asked his father. "I've picked my nose."

"It's not something you want to do in public," said Marvin's mother. "But everyone has done it."

He looked at his mother. "You too?"

"Sometimes a tissue just won't get it," she said. "You blow and you blow, but nothing comes out."

Marvin was horrified.

"I sometimes pick my nose," said Jacob.

"Well, no wonder I pick my nose!" Marvin exclaimed. "I come from a whole family of nose pickers!"

"Your teacher, Mrs. North," said Marvin's father. "I'm sure she's picked her nose before."

"Mrs. North? Are you crazy?"

"The president of the United States has picked his nose," said Marvin's mother.

Marvin looked around the room, from his mother, to his father, to his brother, to his sister.

Either he came from the most disgusting family in the world, or. ... He knew what question he'd ask for the class survey.

Marvin got to school early, and waited.

Judy Jasper was dropped off in the school parking lot. Marvin watched her get out of the car.

Marvin was glad she was alone.

The kids usually weren't mean to him when they were alone. It was only when they were in a group. The bigger the group, the meaner they acted.

"Judy," he called.

"What?" asked Judy.

She had very curly hair.

"I have to ask you my question for the

class survey," said Marvin.

"Okay," said Judy.

"You have to tell the truth," said Marvin.

"I will," said Judy.

"Okay," said Marvin. "Well, here goes." He took a breath. "Have you ever picked your nose?"

Judy screamed, then ran away.

Marvin ran after her. "Wait!" he called. "You have to answer my question!"

He chased her around the bike rack and caught up with her just outside the girls' bathroom.

"Have you ever picked your nose?" he asked again.

"*Ever?*" asked Judy.

Marvin nodded.

Judy ducked into the girls' bathroom.

Marvin was about to walk away.
But then, safe within the bathroom
walls, Judy Jasper shouted, "Yes!"

Kenny was drinking from the water fountain.

"I have to ask you my question for the class survey," said Marvin.

Kenny kept drinking.

"Have you ever picked your nose?" asked Marvin.

Kenny coughed and spit out water. He looked up at Marvin. "That's your question?" he asked.

Marvin nodded.

"Did Mrs. North approve it?"

Marvin shrugged.

"Darn!" said Kenny. "I didn't know you could ask questions like that."

"So, have you?" asked Marvin.

"Yeah, I guess," said Kenny.

Marvin wrote down Kenny's answer.

"I'm going to see if it's too late to change my question," said Kenny. "I could ask all the girls—What color is your underwear?" He cracked up.

Nick and Stuart arrived together.

"What do you want?" asked Nick.

"Don't worry," said Marvin. "I'm not

going to try to be your friend. I just have to ask you my question for the class survey."

"Okay," said Stuart. "But make it quick." He looked around to make sure that no one was watching.

"Have you ever picked your nose?" asked Marvin.

"Give me a break," said Stuart.

"Just answer the question," said Marvin.

"No one's ever going to like you if you keep asking questions like that," said Nick.

"Just answer the question."

"Yes, I've picked my nose," said Stuart. "Are you happy?"

"Me too," said Nick. "But I don't go around talking about it!"

"What do you want, Snot-face?" asked Clarence.

"I have to ask you my survey question."

"Just don't get any of your boogers on me," said Clarence.

Marvin looked at him. He couldn't understand Clarence. They both knew that Clarence made that up. They both knew the ball was over the line.

"No one else is around," said Marvin. "Can't we just be honest with each other?"

"Booger brain!" said Clarence.

"Well, here's my question," said Marvin. "And you have to tell the truth."

"I never lie," said Clarence.

"Have you ever picked your nose?"

"No way!" said Clarence. "I'm not gross like you."

Casey's ponytail stuck out of the side of her head.

"Casey," said Marvin. "I have to ask you my question for the class survey."

"Shoot," said Casey.

"Have you ever picked your nose?"

Casey laughed.

"Well, have you?" asked Marvin.

She laughed so hard she fell to the ground.

Marvin waited patiently.

At last Casey stopped laughing. She took a deep breath. "What was your question?"

"Have you ever picked your nose?" asked Marvin.

She laughed again.

But between her hoots and howls, she managed to shriek, "Yes!"

Justin said, "You're sickening, Marvin!
I'm not going to answer that question."

"You have to," said Marvin. "It's for
the survey."

Justin turned and walked away.

Marvin grabbed his shoulder. "You
have to answer the question."

"Not that question," said Justin, pushing Marvin away.

"You have to!" said Marvin, grabbing him again.

"Justin! Marvin!" shouted Mrs. Grant.

Mrs. Grant was on yard duty. She sent the two boys to see Mr. McCabe, the principal, for fighting.

A little while later, Marvin opened the door to his classroom. He peeked inside. Everyone else was still outside.

"Mrs. North?"

"Yes, Marvin," said his teacher, seated at her desk.

"I want to ask you my question for the class survey."

"Good for you, Marvin. I'm glad to see you're finally participating."

"Have you ever picked your nose?"

Mrs. North sat up straight. "That's no way to talk to a teacher," she said.

"It's for my survey," said Marvin. "Have you ever picked your nose?"

"That is not a proper question," she said. "You need to choose something more appropriate."

"Have you ever picked your nose?" Marvin repeated.

"I'm serious, Marvin," said Mrs. North. "If you ask me that one more time, I'm going to send you straight to the principal's office."

"I just came from there," said Marvin. "Mrs. Grant sent me, for fighting with Justin."

"There, see. And what did Mr. McCabe tell you?"

"He told me he picked his nose."

10

By recess everyone had heard about Marvin's question.

They couldn't wait to answer it.

"Ask me!" said Gina.

"No, ask me," said Heather.

"Okay," said Marvin. "Have you ever picked your nose?"

"Yes," said Gina.

"Yes," said Heather.

Then they ran away giggling.

"Ask me!" said Melanie.

"Ask me!" said Travis ...

After recess Marvin was ready to give his

report. He stood at the front of the room.

Several kids were already snickering.

Marvin began. "As you know, I asked everyone the question—Have you ever picked your nose?"

Everyone cracked up.

Clarence called out, "How gross!"

Marvin waited. "These are the results,"
he said. "Judy—Yes."

The class laughed.

"Kenny—Yes."

They laughed again.

"Stuart—Yes. Nick—Yes. Casey—Yes."

They laughed every time Marvin said, "Yes."

"Justin—Yes. Mr. McCabe—"

There was a gasp. No one knew Marvin had asked the principal.

Marvin paused. Then he said, "Yes."

The class went wild.

Marvin waited for everyone to be quiet. "Mrs. North—"

Again there was a gasp.

"Yes."

"Settle down," said Mrs. North. She was blushing.

Marvin continued. "Travis—Yes. Melanie—Yes. Patsy—Yes. Clarence—No."

Everyone stopped laughing and looked at Clarence.

"Gina—Yes. Heather—Yes."

Marvin finished off the list.

"In summary," he said, "everybody has picked their nose, except Clarence."

Casey shouted, "Oh, Clarence. You're such a liar!"

Mrs. North thanked Marvin for his report. "Excellent job," she said. "It was an unusual question, but I think it taught us all a lot about ourselves. We're all human, aren't we?"

"Way to go, Marvin!" called Stuart.

Nick clapped his hands, and the rest of the class joined in.

After lunch Marvin got on line to play wall-ball. No one complained.

After all, what could they say?

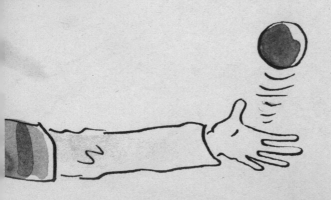

About the Author

Louis Sachar conducted his own "class survey" in order to find the best title for this book. He told the students in the classrooms he visited that he wanted the title to end with a question mark and have the word "pick" in it. Out of all the titles that were suggested, Louis chose "Why Pick on Me?"

Louis Sachar lives in Austin, Texas, with his wife, Carla, and their daughter, Sherre.